D0356163

WELCOME T
PASSPORT TO READING
A beginning reader's ticket to a brand-new world!

Every book in this program is designed to build read-along and read-alone skills, level by level, through engaging and enriching stories. As the reader turns each page, he or she will become more confident with new vocabulary, sight words, and comprehension.

These PASSPORT TO READING levels will help you choose the perfect book for every reader.

READING TOGETHER
Read short words in simple sentence structures together to begin a reader's journey.

READING OUT LOUD
Encourage developing readers to sound out words in more complex stories with simple vocabulary.

READING INDEPENDENTLY
Newly independent readers gain confidence reading more complex sentences with higher word counts.

READY TO READ MORE
Readers prepare for chapter books with fewer illustrations and longer paragraphs.

This book features sight words from the educator-supported Dolch Sight Words List. This encourages the reader to recognize commonly used vocabulary words, increasing reading speed and fluency.

For more information, please visit passporttoreadingbooks.com.

Enjoy the journey!

Little, Brown and Company
Hachette Book Group
1290 Avenue of the Americas, New York, NY 10104
Visit us at LBYR.com
First Edition: February 2019

Little, Brown and Company is a division of Hachette Book Group, Inc.
The Little, Brown name and logo are trademarks of Hachette Book Group, Inc.

The publisher is not responsible for websites (or their content) that are not owned by the publisher.

ISBNs: 978-0-316-41484-5 (pbk.), 978-0-316-41488-3 (ebook), 978-0-316-41486-9 (ebook), 978-0-316-41489-0 (ebook)

PRINTED IN THE UNITED STATES OF AMERICA

CW

10 9 8 7 6 5 4 3 2 1

Passport to Reading titles are leveled by independent reviewers applying the standards developed by Irene Fountas and Gay Su Pinnell in *Matching Books to Readers: Using Leveled Books in Guided Reading*, Heinemann, 1999.

WONDER PARK

A New Adventure!

Story adapted by Trey King

LB

LITTLE, BROWN AND COMPANY
New York   Boston

Attention, WONDER PARK friends!
Look for these words when
you read this book.
Can you spot them all?

pretend

roller coaster

beavers

rocket

"I am not going to go to math camp," says June Bailey.

She wants to stay home
with her dad.
She is worried about
leaving him home alone.

"I am going to be fine,"
June's dad insists.
He wants June to go to
camp and have some fun.

He puts her on the bus.
June tries to look excited.

June and her friend Banky
are heading to math camp.
But after the bus leaves,
June changes her mind.

She has a clever plan.
Banky pretends to be sick.

When the bus driver
pulls over to help him,
June sneaks away.

She knows the way back home.
It is through the woods.
But June follows a different
path and gets lost in the forest.

What is this?

She finds a roller coaster car.

Whoa!

She sits in it.

It starts to move.

The roller coaster car takes her to an old amusement park. June knows this place!

It is just like the park she imagined as a little kid.
She used to play pretend with her mom.
It is so great to see it again!

All of a sudden,
a giant blue bear
runs by.
He looks very scared.

A boar, a porcupine,
and two beavers
also run past June.
They shout, "Run!"
What are they afraid of?

Wonder Chimps?
June knows all about them.
Wonder Chimps are stuffed
animal toys from the park.
But now they are called
Chimpanzombies!

They are after the animals
who live in Wonder Park.
Boomer the bear says,
"We are at war!"

Boomer suddenly falls asleep.

He does this a lot.

This is not a good time for a nap!

The Chimpanzombies throw, crash, blast, and wreck everything they can get their paws on.

Luckily Steve the porcupine has a plan to get rid of them!

The animals trick the Chimpanzombies into entering the Confetti Ship. Greta the boar kicks the door shut.

The beavers, Gus and Cooper,
get the rocket ready to launch.
Then…

...the rocket shoots up, up, up into the sky with the Chimpanzombies inside!

"This cannot be real,"
June says.
But it is real.

But this is also not the park
that June remembers.
"What happened to this place?"
she asks the animals.

"The Darkness happened," Boomer explains.

"It changed the Wonder Chimp dolls into an army of Chimpanzombies. They are tearing apart the park."

The animals want to save the park.
But they do not know how.

Now June is not just
worried about her dad,
she is worried about
her new friends, too!

June thinks she can fix Wonder Park. She is determined to use her ideas to help save the day!